Borah Elementary School
632 Borah
Coeur d' Alene, ID 83814
Ph (208) 664-5844

Motley the Cat

Paintings by Mary Fedden
Story by Susannah Amoore

VIKING

There is a cat called Motley. An enormous striped-like-a-tiger cat with a scarlet collar, glittering lime-green eyes, and great curves of wiry whiskers springing from either side of the widest nose ever seen on a cat. When he stalks into a room there is an immediate hush, then a gasp of astonishment at such splendor and power.

"Look at the size of that incredible cat!" they cry. "Look at the matching stripes up his legs like rugby socks, his lime-green eyes, the length of his whiskers, his nose! Where did he come from?"

"Motley arrived by magic," his family explains. They describe how he prowls along the edge of the river where herons fish when the tide is low – and where branches of willow lean far out to dip their leaves in the olive-green water that is sliding by with its cargoes of ducks and mysterious fish.

Motley likes to chase rats: long, strong, riverside rats. With powerful claws ready, he shoulders his way through tall tangles of cow-parsley. He catapults out, so pleased with himself and his life, with seeds on his whiskers and his shining tiger-striped coat powdered with white from pollen and petals.

Now and again he will sniff the breeze for the faintest whiff of his favorite enemy cats – the black with no tail, the detested long-haired ginger-and-white – who are nicely tough and brave in just the way the best sort of enemy cat must be.

They rarely fight. But they meet later at night, those promising hours for cats on adventures. With bristling fur, stiffened slow-moving legs, and some impressive hissing and yowling, they take it in turns to menace and stalk each other beneath the cool-shadowed moonlight, while the river beside them flows silver and dark and fast.

B ut Motley's most important adventure began one beautiful midsummer's day, a day so hot that the birds were quiet. A mighty leap to the top of a high brick wall, and he was on his way to the green where the great lime trees grow and lean so close that it is hard to tell in a summer breeze if a certain branch belongs to this tree or that tree.

T wo little girls were in the garden, that day, of a very tall house with a blue front door on the edge of the green. They were sleepily reading in the shade of lengthening shadows of trees.

Darius, their beloved ink-black cat, had vanished into cooler deep-green bushes. He loved to lie on his back and pat at moths that fluttered just out of reach of his paws in the bright blue air above him. He longed for mouthfuls of moth.

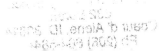

The girls couldn't know, but the magic had started. Motley was running toward them and into their lives along the top of the high brick wall that led to their garden.

He approached very quietly; they heard nothing. But the garden felt suddenly altered, tilted, as if some unusual force was around. They looked up sharply and saw an enormous tiger-striped cat staring down with gleaming lime-green eyes. It was the largest, the ugliest, and yet the most beautiful cat ever seen. A cat who must surely be loved, since he was wearing a scarlet collar with a silvery disk.

The girls jumped up, and almost at once the cat was butting and purring and trampling all over them in frenzied excitement as they tried to catch hold of the silvery disk. MOTLEY, it read, THE COLLEGE OF ADULT EDUCATION.

The family was bewitched by the ferocious charm of this striped-like-a-tiger enchanter who had wandered so far from home. Joyful, he stayed overnight in that very tall house and leaped onto knees with road-digger purrs. But when the children played cards, his eyes turned a darkened, frightening, glittery green as he tensed and threatened and suddenly sprang at their slippery piles of diamonds and hearts, clubs and spades.

COLLEG
ADULT EDUC

In the morning, the girls and their mother pushed a struggling Motley into Darius's big wicker basket and hauled him back to his college. The caretaker, sweeping the path, saw an outraged tigerlike face through the grille of the basket.

"Not him again!" he shouted. "This time I thought he'd found what he goes looking for – a real home. Why don't you keep him? I don't want him!"

Opening the basket, the girls said they already had a cat, an elderly cat they loved. "We have to leave Motley behind, so please will you look after him still?"

Then Motley, oh so glad to be freed, burst from the basket and fled inside.

Nearly a year went by, and no one forgot that enormous beautiful-ugly striped-like-a-tiger enchanter. But there was no sign of him, no tilt of the garden, no hint in the distance of the magic at work.

The little girls would gaze out of the windows hoping for even a glimpse of tigerlike stripes on far-off bends of the wall. But he was never seen.

"Motley must have found what he was looking for," their mother said. "A home of his own. I am glad!" They smiled (and sighed) and agreed how lucky they were, the people he had found, to have their address on his silvery disk.

B ut they were to sigh even more toward the end of that year. Darius, their own beloved ink-black cat, was now very old and became ill and lost interest in eating.

At first they were just worried, then filled with a terrible sadness when the vet took him gently away. The girls and their mother, with tears in their eyes, down their cheeks, on their chins, walked home over the green, carrying the empty basket.

But then something extraordinary happened, something hard to explain.

When they went through the blue front door and into the living room, one of the girls cried, "Look!" And the room felt suddenly altered, a little skew-whiff, as if it were somehow holding its breath.

They looked where she pointed, and there, pressed to the glass of the window, was that face, that unforgettable face. A face with great curves of wiry whiskers attached at the sides. An enormous beautiful-ugly striped-like-a-tiger face. A face with shining lime-green eyes set on either side of the widest nose they ever remembered.

N ow laughing and crying together, the girls pulled open the door, and Motley, with eyes turned a most brilliant triumphant green, came swaggering grandly into the room and into their lives forever.

Somewhere out of sight, but keeping watch and knowing everything, Motley had waited nearly a year for the vacancy. And being a cat of quite exceptional power and magic, his arrival was timed exactly right.